My Name Is Bilal

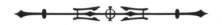

My Name Is Bilal

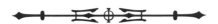

by Asma Mobin-Uddin • *Illustrated by* Barbara Kiwak

BOYDS MILLS PRESS

An Imprint of Highlights
Honesdale, Pennsylvania

The author wishes to thank Greg Linder, editor, for all his assistance with this manuscript.

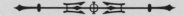

Published by Boyds Mills Press, Inc.

A Highlights Company

815 Church Street

Honesdale, Pennsylvania 18431

Printed in China

Visit our website at boydsmillspress.com

Library of Congress Cataloging-in-Publication Data

Mobin-Uddin, Asma.

  My name is Bilal / by Asma Mobin-Uddin ; illustrated by Barbara Kiwak.— 1st ed.

    p. cm.

  Summary: When Bilal and his sister transfer to a school where they are the only Muslims, they must
learn how to fit in while staying true to their beliefs and heritage.

  ISBN 1-59078-175-9 (alk. paper)

  [1. Muslims—Fiction. 2. Prejudices—Fiction. 3. Schools—Fiction.] I. Kiwak, Barbara, ill. II. Title.

PZ7.M71273My 2005   [Fic]—dc22

                                        2004029069

First edition, 2005

The text of this book is set in Minion.

The illustrations are done in watercolor.

10 9 8 7 6 5 4

In memory of my father
—AM-U

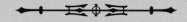

To Lynn
—BK

AYESHA'S WHITE SCARF DRAPED GRACEFULLY over her head and shoulders. From the parking lot of their new school, Bilal saw that none of the other students were dressed like his sister. Suddenly he felt afraid. Ayesha clutched her notebook to her chest, showing that she, too, was afraid. But she was smiling as she walked toward the school building. A gust of wind blew Bilal's cap off his head.

"Do you need help?" Ayesha called as he ran after it.

"No. I'll get it," called Bilal. "You go ahead."

Ayesha nodded and turned toward the school, ignoring the stares and whispers of the other children.

Bilal's cap came to rest in some bushes behind a tree in the schoolyard. As he bent to pick it up, he saw two boys following Ayesha.

ONE OF THE BOYS GRABBED HER HEADSCARF and tugged on it. When Ayesha spun around, the boy let go. He and his friend ran off laughing. Other students giggled at Ayesha's lopsided scarf.

Bilal stood frozen behind the tree, unable to run to his sister's side. His heart was pounding. Then he heard the school bell ring. Bilal wished his family had never left Chicago. At his old school, there had been lots of Muslim kids. Here, it seemed there were none.

The cold, hard windows of the new school glared at him. He knew he had to go inside. Bilal bowed his head and shuffled up the empty sidewalk.

BILAL FOUND THE CLASSROOM HE HAD VISITED with his parents the week before. He sat down without looking at anyone.

"Class, we have been joined by a new student," the teacher announced. Twenty-four pairs of eyes turned to look at Bilal. Bilal looked up. The bully who had pulled Ayesha's scarf was staring at him. Again, Bilal felt afraid. Had the boy seen him walking with Ayesha?

Mr. Ali, the teacher, was calling his name. "Bilal. Bilal?"

Bilal spoke at last. "Al is my middle name," he stammered. "My first name is Bill."

Mr. Ali looked at him for a long moment. "Class, I want you all to introduce yourselves to . . . Bill," he said. One by one, the students stood up and said their names.

"Scott," the bully said when it was his turn. He scowled at Bilal, and he did not stand up.

Mr. Ali began talking about an assignment. Bilal tried to pay attention, but all he could think about was Scott's mean stare and the way Scott had laughed at his sister. Bilal did not even dare to look at him.

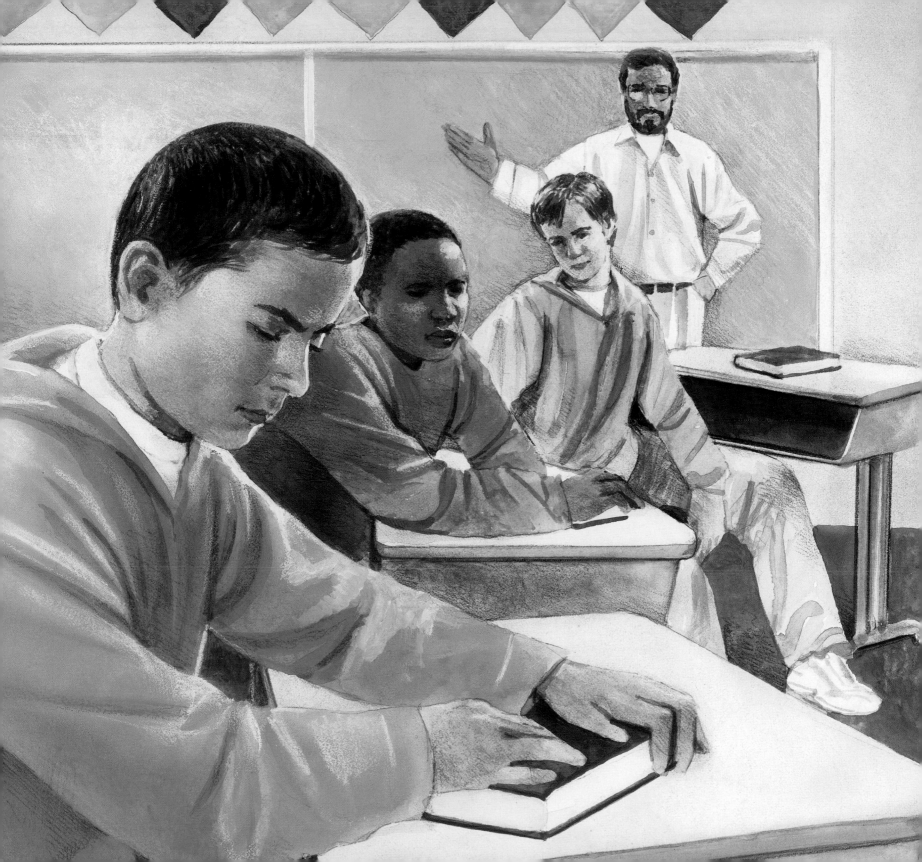

AS SOON AS CLASS WAS OVER, Bilal tried to slip out of the room. Mr. Ali called to him before he could reach the door. As the other students filed past him, Bilal slowly turned and approached his teacher's desk.

"Peace be upon you," Mr. Ali said. This was the traditional Muslim greeting, and he spoke in the Arabic language. Bilal had heard these words every day of his life. Today, though, he looked around to be certain the room was empty before he replied.

"And peace be upon you," he said.

"I enjoyed having dinner with your family last night," the teacher told Bilal. "The last time I saw your father was thirty years ago, long before either one of us came to the United States."

"Yes, sir." Bilal knew this. His father loved to tell stories about his school days with Mr. Ali.

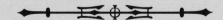

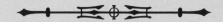

NOW THE TEACHER LEANED FORWARD to look at Bilal. "Son, why did you say your name was Bill?"

"Because I want to be like everybody else. Nobody else in the class has a name like Bilal."

"But Bilal is a common name for Muslim boys," Mr. Ali said. Bilal looked down at the floor. "I don't want anyone to know I'm Muslim," he said, almost whispering. "You won't tell anyone, will you?"

The teacher stood up. "I will keep your secret," Mr. Ali said kindly. "But I have a book that I would like you to read. You can do a book report on it. Can you come with your father to evening prayers at the mosque tonight?"

Bilal nodded.

"I will give the book to you then."

That evening, as his father sat reading the Qur'an in the mosque, Bilal looked for his teacher. When he found him, Bilal stared in surprise at the title of the book Mr. Ali was holding: *Bilal Ibn Rabah, Friend and Helper of the Prophet.*

"I've never heard of anyone famous named Bilal!" he said.

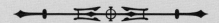

"BILAL IBN RABAH WAS THE FIRST PERSON to give the Muslim call to prayer during the time of Prophet Muhammad, peace be upon him. Bilal lived about fourteen hundred years ago," Mr. Ali said. "He would climb to the top of the mosque and recite the *adhan*. His strong and faithful voice reminded Muslims to pray throughout the day."

"It must have been easy to be a Muslim back then," Bilal said. "Things are different now."

Mr. Ali shook his head. "Life was hard for the early Muslims, too, Bilal. People in Mecca hurt them and tried to make them forget God. But Bilal and the early Muslims knew it was more important to please God than to please the people."

"What did the people in Mecca do to Bilal?"

"Find out," Mr. Ali said, handing him the book.

As Bilal turned to leave, the gentle sound of the call to prayer filled the mosque. *God is the greatest. God is the greatest* . . . the Arabic words began. Bilal watched people line up for prayer. He rarely prayed at the mosque.

Come to prayer . . . the voice beckoned. Bilal decided to stand in line beside Mr. Ali. Maybe God would help him feel less afraid.

THAT NIGHT, BILAL READ FROM MR. ALI'S BOOK.
Bilal Ibn Rabah was a slave whose family came from the ancient land of Abyssinia, near where Ethiopia is today. He became a Muslim in the Arabian city of Mecca. The people of Mecca tormented Bilal by throwing him to the ground and placing heavy rocks on his chest. They said they would stop if he would agree to worship their gods.

Each time they put another rock on him, Bilal would say, "One, one." It was his way of telling them that there was only one God, and that he remained God's servant. Bilal laid back on his pillow, thinking about what he had read.

Bilal FELT A CRUSHING PAIN ON HIS CHEST. The rocks were heavy. They were hot from the desert sun. His skin was coated with sweat, and he could scarcely breathe. Bilal heard voices chanting, "Change your name and we will stop."

In his dream, Bilal was calm. "My name is Bilal. I am a Muslim," he told the angry people. Despite the pain, he knew that he had nothing to fear, for he was pleasing God. Bilal awakened with a start. His room was dark and cool, but the dream was still with him.

AT SCHOOL THE NEXT MORNING, Bilal saw Scott standing in front of Ayesha's locker. The boy wore a T-shirt draped over his head. When Ayesha approached her locker, Scott turned to a friend and spoke in a loud voice.

"I got a terrible haircut yesterday," he said. "Now I have to wear this T-shirt on my head until my hair grows out." His friend burst out laughing. So did some of the students in the hallway.

Ayesha stopped at her locker. "While you're waiting for your hair to grow, would you please move away from my locker?" A few of the students giggled.

Scott pulled the shirt off his head and glared at Ayesha. "This is America," he growled. "We don't wear dumb things on our heads."

"If this is America, I can wear what I want," Ayesha said, lifting her head defiantly. "And I want to cover my hair. Now please move!"

"She wants to cover her hair." Scott told his friend. "Maybe we were wrong. Maybe she's not bald after all!"

Bilal hurried to his sister's side. "Leave her alone, Scott," he said firmly. Scott and his friend stopped laughing.

"What do you care, Bill?" Scott demanded. "She's weird. She should go back to her own country!" The hallway was silent. Every pair of eyes was watching Bilal, Scott, and Ayesha.

Bilal took a deep breath. "My name is not Bill. It's Bilal. My sister and I are Muslims," he said, stepping between Scott and Ayesha. "And America *is* our country. We were born here."

A school bell shattered the silence. Students walked away without another word. Soon Bilal and Ayesha stood alone in the hallway.

"Ayesha," Bilal said to his sister, "I'm sorry I didn't stand up for you yesterday, when that boy pulled on your scarf."

"It's okay," Ayesha replied with a smile. "I'm glad you were on my side today."

As they turned to leave, Bilal caught sight of Mr. Ali standing in a classroom door. From Mr. Ali's expression, Bilal knew he had seen everything. Bilal smiled at his teacher, who responded with a nod and a thumbs-up sign.

AFTER SCHOOL, BILAL JOINED SOME BOYS who were playing basketball at a nearby park. Bilal ran up and down the court, passed the ball to his teammates, and shot at the basket. The rhythm of the game helped him forget the trouble at school. But not for long.

Bilal saw a boy standing behind the fence, frowning at him. The boy was Scott.

For a few minutes, Bilal ignored him. Then a new game started. Bilal walked over to the fence.

"Scott, do you want to play?" he asked. "You can be on my team."

Scott looked surprised. His frown faded a little. "I guess so," he said. "But I can't stay very long."

Bilal dribbled the ball down the court and took a shot. It arced toward the basket but bounced high off the rim — right back into Bilal's hands. Bilal saw Scott standing near the basket. He pushed a bounce pass to his teammate, and Scott scored an easy lay-up. Two points!

As they ran back down the court, Scott caught up with Bilal. "Nice pass, Bill!" he said. "I mean . . . Bilal."

Bilal grinned. "Great shot!" he told Scott.

WHEN THE GAME WAS OVER, one of the older boys stopped playing. "I need to take a break," he said. "I'll be back in a few minutes." He walked off the court.

"I have to go, too," Scott said. "I'll see you in school tomorrow, Bilal."

Bilal waved at Scott and smiled. Then he asked a teammate where the older boy had gone. "He's Muslim," the boy said. "He always prays in the afternoon."

Bilal stared at the boy in surprise. "You don't mind that he stops to pray?"

"Nope. It gives me more time to practice," the boy answered.

BILAL CAUGHT UP WITH THE OLDER BOY.
"Peace be upon you!" he said.

"And peace be upon you. I'm Hakim." Hakim held out his hand, and Bilal shook it.

"My name is . . . Bilal." The simple words seemed to come from his heart. Saying his name made him feel strong. "Let's pray together," he said.

The two boys washed for prayer at a drinking fountain. Hakim took a prayer rug from his duffel bag and spread it on the ground.

Bilal stood beneath a clear blue sky as Hakim sat beside him. The autumn sun shone warmly, and a gentle breeze cooled their faces. A quiet feeling of peace settled over Bilal.

With a voice carried to the hills by the wind, for Hakim and for himself, Bilal gave the call to prayer.

Author's Notes

Muslims pray a special type of prayer, called *salat* (suh-LAAT), at five specified times throughout the day. Before the prayer, the *adhan* (uh-THAN), or call to prayer, is recited in the Arabic language. Here is an English translation of the adhan:

God is the greatest. God is the greatest.
God is the greatest. God is the greatest.
I bear witness that nothing deserves to be worshipped except God.
I bear witness that nothing deserves to be worshipped except God.
I bear witness that Muhammad is the messenger of God.
I bear witness that Muhammad is the messenger of God.
Come to prayer. Come to prayer.
Come to success. Come to success.
God is greatest. God is greatest.
Nothing deserves to be worshipped except God.

The traditional Muslim greeting is the Arabic phrase *As-salaamu alaykum* (us-suh-LAM-u ah-LAY-kum), which means *Peace be upon you.*

The reply is *Wa alaykum as-salaam* (wuh ah-LAY-kum us-suh-LAM), which means *And peace be upon you.*

The name Muhammad is also commonly spelled Mohammad. I have chosen the former spelling because it is phonetically closer to the Arabic.